Read-Along

Read-Along

Cooped up like a prisoner inside Tweedy's Farm, a chicken named Ginger dreams of the impossible: wide open spaces, grass beneath her feet, and a chance to do more than meet the daily egg quota.

Join Ginger and her fellow hens in their quest for freedom. When you hear this sound, turn the page.

As night falls, Ginger makes her latest daring escape attempt. She dashes across the barnyard to the barbed wire fence, whips out a spoon, and starts digging. When the hole is big enough, she crawls under the fence. At her signal, five other hens rush out from the shadows. Bunty, the biggest bird of them all, climbs into the hole. The hens are almost home free. But Bunty gets stuck! As the hens push and pull at Bunty, Mr. Tweedy catches Ginger outside the fence. Before she can get away, he scoops her up and dumps her into the coal bin for a night of solitary confinement.

Ginger is released just in time for morning roll call.
Mr. Tweedy boots her into the chicken yard, where
she's greeted by silly Babs. Fowler, the farm's resident
rooster, calls the chickens to attention. As soon as
they are assembled, Mr. and Mrs. Tweedy begin the
daily egg count. But one hen, Edwina,
hasn't laid any for three days straight!
Ginger and the other hens look on help-
lessly as Edwina is

taken away by Mr. Tweedy. At Tweedy's, if you're not a layer, you're dinner.

Now Ginger is more determined than ever to escape. That night, she calls a secret meeting of the escape committee to discuss new plans.

At the escape committee meeting, Ginger and
Mac—chief engineer and Ginger's right-hand hen—
demonstrate the latest plan with the help of a turnip.
They'll build a catapult and go *over* the fence. The
room fills with nervous clucking as the turnip smashes
against the wall. This is the craziest plan yet! Maybe
they should just accept their lot in life.

Ginger tries to rally them, but she fears she'll never
be able to lead her fine feathered friends to freedom.
What she needs now is a miracle.

Discouraged, Ginger leaves the hut. Suddenly, she hears a shout. She looks up to see a rooster flying through the air. He crash-lands in the barnyard, and a piece of a poster advertising "Rocky the Flying Rooster" floats down after him. Ginger's heart soars as she gazes at the poster. She's hatched a new plan.

The hens rush Rocky inside and bandage his sprained wing as Ginger explains her idea. Rocky will teach them to fly. But Rocky's plans don't include sticking around a chicken farm.

Rocky is about to leave when a circus van pulls up. He's on the run from the circus! Thinking quickly, Ginger makes a deal: The hens will hide Rocky, if he teaches them how to fly. Rocky has no choice but to help them out.

The next morning, Rocky begins training the flock. The hens all work hard to get in shape, but after a few days, no one has lifted a feather off the ground. As Nick and Fetcher, the farmyard rats, laugh at their failed attempts, Ginger starts to have a sinking feeling about Rocky.

Meanwhile, strange things are happening on the farm. A truck delivers a huge crate. Mrs. Tweedy starts measuring the chickens instead of counting eggs. Then the food rations are doubled, sending the hens into an eating frenzy. Finally, Ginger gets the picture. Mrs. Tweedy is fattening them up! She's going to kill them all. But how?

Rocky comes up with a plan of his own. He decides that the chickens need a little fun to cheer them up. By promising Nick and Fetcher the next egg he lays, Rocky cons the two sneaky rats into stealing a radio. But Nick and Fetcher will be waiting a long time for their payback—roosters don't lay eggs!

Soon the hens are tapping their toes and moving to the music. Even Ginger takes a turn with Rocky on the dance floor. With all the flapping and twirling, Babs suddenly goes airborne! Her flight only lasts a moment, but it renews the chickens' hope. During all the commotion, Ginger notices that Rocky's wing is better. Now Rocky can demonstrate his flying technique. Rocky is about to tell Ginger the truth about his flying skills, when suddenly a deafening rumble is heard from the barn.

Mr. and Mrs. Tweedy have just turned on their new money-making investment—a pie machine, for chicken pies. Soon every store in the county will be stocked with Mrs. Tweedy's Homemade Chicken Pies. But first the machine must be tested. Before she can shake a feather, Ginger is snapped up, strapped onto a conveyer belt, and headed straight into the belly of the beast!

Fearlessly, Rocky charges into the pie machine after her. Dodging mixed vegetables and rotating saw blades, he finds Ginger, and they make their escape—but not before sabotaging the machine.

Back in the hut, Ginger tells the hens about the ter-
rible pie-making machine. The chickens start to panic.
But Ginger calms them down with the news that
Rocky will show them how to fly tomorrow. Soon
they'll be free!

Later Ginger thanks Rocky for saving her life.
Rocky tries once again to tell her his secret, but he
just can't get the words out.

The hens can't wait to see Rocky fly. But when Ginger goes to find Rocky the next morning, his bunk is empty. All that's left is the bottom half of Rocky's poster. It shows him being fired out of a circus cannon. Ginger realizes the truth. Rocky couldn't fly after all! Her hopes dashed, she breaks the bad news to the hens.

Without Ginger's dreams to guide them, the hens begin to squabble—and the squabble turns into an all-out mud fight. As Fowler steps in to break it up, Ginger realizes something. Fowler was in the RAF—the Royal Air Force! Filled with inspiration, Ginger devises a new plan. They'll build an airplane—just like the one Fowler flew!

With no time to lose, the hens get organized.
Everyone lends a hand. In exchange for eggs from
Bunty, Nick and Fetcher help the chickens steal tools
right out from under Mr. Tweedy's nose. Seeing the
hens so energized fills Ginger with pride. But it also
makes her realize something. She misses Rocky.

Meanwhile, out on his own, Rocky is realizing something, too. Freedom can be a lonely road to follow. Spotting a huge billboard advertising Mrs. Tweedy's chicken pies, Rocky begins to question his decision to leave Ginger and the other hens in their time of need.

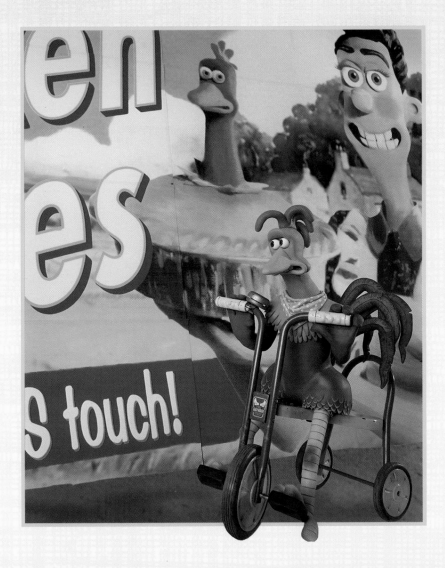

Back in the barnyard, the chickens freeze in fear as the repaired pie machine roars to life again. When Mr. Tweedy comes to get them, Ginger and the hens swoop down and overpower him. They truss him up like a stuffed bird and wheel the flying machine out onto a runway lit by a string of Christmas lights. The time has come to make their escape!

But there's just one problem: Fowler has never flown a plane before! He was a mascot in the RAF—not a pilot. Ginger convinces him to take the controls. As the plane approaches the takeoff ramp, Mr. Tweedy jumps up and kicks it over. Then Mrs. Tweedy appears, and looms over Ginger with an ax. But before she can swing, a loud noise distracts her.

It's Rocky! Riding a tricycle! He speeds downhill, sails over the fence, and knocks Mrs. Tweedy to the ground. Rocky and Ginger quickly put the ramp in place and the plane takes off, trailing the Christmas lights behind it. Rocky and Ginger grab hold of the lights and climb aboard. Annoyed at Rocky for leaving, Ginger slaps him. Then, happy to have him back, she leans over and gives him a kiss.

As she does, the plane jolts. Mrs. Tweedy has grabbed hold of the lights. Ginger leans out to cut the string of lights, and before she knows it, she and Mrs. Tweedy are dangling behind the plane. As Ginger tries to cut Mrs. Tweedy off, she's hit in the face with something. It's an egg! Rocky is attacking Mrs. Tweedy with the help of Nick and Fetcher.

But they don't have enough eggs! Mrs. Tweedy swings the ax at Ginger. Just in time, Ginger ducks. The ax slices through the string of lights, sending Mrs. Tweedy tumbling down—through the roof of the barn and into the pie machine.

The plane soars up and away from the barn. Meanwhile, Mrs. Tweedy tries to escape from the pie machine.

But before Mr. Tweedy can free her, the machine explodes! Mrs. Tweedy is swept up in a flood of gravy—unharmed yet unhappy. Her pie machine is ruined, her dreams have been dashed, and her chickens are gone.

And yes, Rocky, Ginger, and the others finally make it to freedom. Proving once and for all that a little luck and a lot of pluck go a long way.

PUFFIN BOOKS
Published by the Penguin Group
Penguin Putnam Books for Young Readers,
345 Hudson Street, New York, New York 10014, U.S.A.
Penguin Books Ltd, 27 Wrights Lane, London W8 5TZ, England
Penguin Books Australia Ltd, Ringwood, Victoria, Australia
Penguin Books Canada Ltd, 10 Alcorn Avenue, Toronto, Ontario, Canada M4V 3B2
Penguin Books (N.Z.) Ltd, 182-190 Wairau Road, Auckland 10, New Zealand

Penguin Books Ltd, Registered Offices: Harmondsworth, Middlesex, England

Published by Puffin Books,
a division of Penguin Putnam Books for Young Readers, 2000

1 3 5 7 9 10 8 6 4 2

TM & © 2000 DreamWorks,
Aardman Chicken Run Limited and Pathè Image.
All rights reserved

Puffin Books ISBN 0-14-099838-1

Printed in the United States of America